Say What?

A Jammin' Fill-in Story

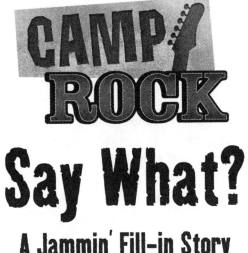

Say What?

A Jammin' Fill-in Story

By Avery Scott

Based on "Camp Rock," Written by Karin Gist & Regina Hicks and Julie Brown & Paul Brown

New York

AN IMPRINT OF DISNEY BOOK GROUP

Instructions

Need a refresher course on what to say? Here's a list of what's what in the world of grammar!

An adjective helps describe a person or a thing. Some examples are: **funny**, **cute**, **stylish**, and **loopy**.

To explain how something is done, use an adverb. Just a hint, they usually end in -ly. Some examples are: **finally**, **loudly**, **excitedly**, and **wickedly**.

A noun is a person, place, or thing. Pretty simple, huh? Some nouns to keep you jammin' are: **guitar**, **microphone**, **bunk**, and **field**.

If you want to put some action into the stories, you need to use a verb. Some examples are: **sing**, **dance**, **swim**, and **play**. Verbs can also be in the past tense, like **rocked**, **walked**, and **dreamed** or they can end in -ing, like **snoozing**, **living**, and **cheering**.

What are you waiting for? Put down your guitar, grab a pencil, and rock on!

Camp Rock Rocks!

Live your Dreams at Camp Rock! Camp Rock is a(n)

_____ musical experience! Suited for both
ADJECTIVE

_____ and experts, Camp Rock will
PLURAL NOUN

make your rock n' roll _____ come true!
PLURAL NOUN

It is _____ 's premiere _____
COUNTRY   NOUN

camp, offering _____ a once in
PLURAL NOUN

a lifetime chance to _____!
VERB

This summer, Camp Rock features _____
CELEBRITY

and _____ as guest instructors.
PERSON IN ROOM

* You must be _____ or
NUMBER

older to _____ at Camp Rock.
VERB

* _____ not provided.
PLURAL NOUN

Campaign Camp Rock

Dear Mom and Dad,

I would like to point out that summer is _____
ADVERB

approaching. But all is not _____! There is still
ADJECTIVE

time for you to make my _____ come true.
PLURAL NOUN

It could be a Camp Rock summer! All you have to do is sign

your _____ on the dotted line and send them a
NOUN

check for the low price of $ _____. Just think of
NUMBER

it as an investment in my _____.
NOUN

Love,

Your _____ daughter, Mitchie
ADJECTIVE

P.S. I will take out the _____ and wash the
NOUN

_____ every day!!
PLURAL NOUN

And the Answer Is?

Hey Mitchie,

Did you get a chance to _____ with your parents
                              VERB

last night? Are they going to let you _____
                                            VERB

at Camp Rock this summer or what? I mean, it's *the*

camp for _____ who love music, like
              PLURAL NOUN

you do. By the end of the summer you'd have

_____ new skills. Maybe you'll even get to
    ADJECTIVE

meet _____! I'd miss you, of course, but I know
        CELEBRITY

Camp Rock will make you feel _____, so I hope
                                    ADVERB

your 'rents said _____! I'm going to be busy
                    SILLY WORD

studying _____ all summer to make sure I get
              SUBJECT

straight _____!
              PLURAL NOUN

Your friend,

Sierra

Camp Rock's a No Go

Hey Sierra,

Sorry to report that Steve and Connie (aka Mom and Dad) said Camp Rock is a no-go. They said things are too busy at the _____,
NAME OF BUSINESS

and Mom is still trying to get the catering company started. Looks like I'll be _____ here
VERB ENDING IN "ING"

in good ole' _____ all summer,
PLACE

flipping _____. But at least I get
TYPE OF FOOD (PLURAL)

to _____ with you! Come find me after
VERB

your last final—I need you to help me clean out

my _____.
NOUN

Later,

M

Camp Rock's a Go!

Hi Dad,

I know it's super soon to be _____, but

VERB ENDING IN "ING"

I'm so excited, I couldn't _____ any longer.

VERB

Mom and I are here at Camp Rock! That's right—Connie's

Catering has arrived! I can't believe the _____

OCCUPATION

of the camp hired mom—and that I got to come

with her! It's already _____, Dad. This is going

ADJECTIVE

to be the most _____ summer ever!

ADJECTIVE ENDING IN "ING"

_____! When we pulled up in the catering

SILLY WORD

truck, there were already _____ singing

PLURAL NOUN

a cappella. Thanks again for letting me come here. We'll talk

to you _____!

ADVERB

Love you,

Mitchie

Who's Who?

Hey Sierra,

Camp Rock has so many groups of _____.
PLURAL NOUN
It's

just like being at _____!
PLACE
There's a group of

kids that like to _____ out to bands like
VERB

The _____.
ANIMAL (PLURAL)
There are some kids that like

_____, kids who like to listen to hip hop,
NOUN

and then other kids who like to listen to alternative

_____.
NOUN
It's a _____ mix! I wonder
ADJECTIVE

where I'll fit in . . . .

Your pal,

Mitchie

Back to Work!

Dear _____,
PERSON IN ROOM (PLURAL)

Yet another summer at Camp Rock has _____
ADVERB

begun, and I think it could be the best one ever!

I know the food will taste _____, that's
ADJECTIVE

for sure. I met the new _____, Connie Torres,
OCCUPATION

today. She seems _____, and her
ADJECTIVE

_____ is out of this world.
TYPE OF FOOD

It'll be a _____ change from the weird
ADJECTIVE

_____ that _____ used to serve
TYPE OF FOOD   CELEBRITY

up! I'm waiting for Shane to arrive any _____.
NOUN

The campers are going to _____ when they
VERB

see him!

Rock on,

Brown

11

You've Been Warned

To Whom It May Concern:

In light of recent _____, _____
                     PLURAL NOUN   COLOR

Records is placing Mr. Shane Gray of Connect

_____ on contractual probation. The stipulations
   NUMBER

of Mr. Gray's probation require him to _____
                                              VERB

at Camp Rock, located in _____, for the
                            COUNTRY

duration of its summer program. _____
                                    SAME COLOR

Records reserves the right to _____ Mr. Gray's
                                 VERB

contract, rendering it null and _____ if Mr.
                                    NOUN

Gray does not fulfill this obligation.

Sincerely,

_____
  CELEBRITY

President of A & R

_____ Records
  SAME COLOR

Queen Bees

Dear Sierra,

Why is it that everywhere I _____, there are
                              VERB

always a group of _____ who think
                    PLURAL NOUN

they're so _____? I think of them as Queen
             ADJECTIVE

_____ because they _____
INSECT (PLURAL)   VERB

insects. They are just so _____ with
                            ADJECTIVE

their shiny _____ and expensive
              PLURAL NOUN

_____. Sometimes I wish they would
ARTICLE OF CLOTHING (PLURAL)

just buzz off!

Sigh,

Mitchie

Pump Up the Jams!

Dear Dee,

Are you ready for another rocking summer at Camp Rock?

Before the _____ arrive and things get
　　　　　　　　　PLURAL NOUN

_____, I wanted to give you the list of some of
　　ADJECTIVE

the _____ I've planned.
　　　PLURAL NOUN

Opening _____ Jam: An
　　　　　　　　NOUN

_____ microphone event.
　　ADJECTIVE

_____ Jam: One big
ARTICLE OF CLOTHING

_____ party set to music.
SAME ARTICLE OF CLOTHING

Final Jam: The culmination of all the _____
　　　　　　　　　　　　　　　　　　　　ADJECTIVE

work the _____ have done.
　　　　　PLURAL NOUN

What do you think?

Brown

We're Here!

Dear Steve,

Mitchie and I are _____ settling in at
                         ADVERB

Camp Rock. I met the camp _____ today.
                              OCCUPATION

His name is Brown, and he was the founding member

of a band called the Wet _____. He wears
                             ANIMAL (PLURAL)

_____ and loves his faded
ARTICLE OF CLOTHING (PLURAL)

_____. I think he wears them every
        PLURAL NOUN

_____. He also tells _____ stories
        NOUN   ADJECTIVE

about the _____ he's toured with in the
              PLURAL NOUN

past. Mitchie is going to be _____ with
                              VERB ENDING IN "ING"

some real pros.

Love you!

Connie

Sign Me Up!

To all Rock-Stars-in-_____ at Camp Rock:
                          VERB ENDING IN "ING"

Registration for this summer's various _____
                                         PLURAL NOUN

will be held tomorrow. If you want to get your first

choice, don't be _____ . Here
                              ADJECTIVE

is the schedule:

Last _____ beginning with A—N:
          PLURAL NOUN

_____ a.m.
     NUMBER

Last _____ beginning with O—Z: 1 p.m.
          PLURAL NOUN

Please arrive with your top _____ choices in
                                  NUMBER

_____ .
       NOUN

Good luck!

Camp Director Brown

Guest Instructor

_____ Campers:
EXCLAMATION

This summer, we will have a guest _____ from
PLURAL NOUN

the _____ industry! This mystery person
NOUN

will share his or her _____ and join you
PLURAL NOUN

in the _____ for _____. You will have
PLACE   TYPE OF FOOD

a chance to _____ him or her questions and
VERB

_____ the inside scoop on life in the business.
VERB

Have fun!

Dee

First Day

Hey Sierra,

I don't have a lot of time to _____, cause I'm
                                    VERB

due at the _____ soon. But I just had to tell you
              NOUN

what happened. I managed to _____ right
                                  VERB

into a girl named Tess Tyler. I wasn't looking where I was

_____, and I was so embarrassed! It turns
VERB ENDING IN "ING"

out that Tess' mom is the _____ time Grammy
                              NUMBER

winner T.J. Tyler! Tess reminds me of _____
                                            CELEBRITY

or _____ back at home. She has
      PERSON IN ROOM (FEMALE)

_____ hair and she's really _____!
      COLOR   ADJECTIVE

She is definitely the _____ of Camp Rock.
                          NOUN

More later,

M

Greetings from Camp Rock

Dear _____,
PERSON IN ROOM

I met this girl named Mitchie today. I'm going to show her the

_____. She seems really _____
PLURAL NOUN   ADJECTIVE

and down to _____. I haven't heard her
PLACE

_____ yet but she has to be pretty good if she's
NOUN

here. I already warned her about Tess Tyler. Remember Tess?

She and I used to _____ together, but then she
VERB

got _____ when I got more attention. Anyway,
ADJECTIVE

hopefully I can save Mitchie from Tess's _____
ADJECTIVE

grasp.

Cheers,

Caitlyn

Guess Who?

Hi _____,

I really do love my job as Camp _____. It's
OCCUPATION

just so _____! Like, today, when I welcomed
ADJECTIVE

in all the new _____ for the summer. You
PLURAL NOUN

know how I _____ explain to them that camp is
ADVERB

not just about Final Jam? Well, this time, I got to share with

them that the _____ pop star, Shane Gray,
ADJECTIVE

is going to be a guest _____! I thought
OCCUPATION

the campers were going to cause a _____, they
NOUN

were so excited!

Hope your tour is going well!

Dee

Shane's Drop-off

Yo _____,
       PLURAL NOUN

I cannot believe you dumped me out of the limo like a

sack of _____! I'm still a member of
              PLURAL NOUN

Connect _____, you know! Now, not only do
              NUMBER

I have to spend the summer _____ at this
                            VERB ENDING IN "ING"

_____ camp (dudes, I thought we were done
    ADJECTIVE

with this _____!), but you have totally
              PLACE

abandoned me! I don't want to hear any more nonsense

about building you a _____ house. And what
                          ANIMAL

was that you said about _____ with the
                         VERB ENDING IN "ING"

winner of Final Jam? I never agreed to that! I'm calling our

_____!
   OCCUPATION

Text me later,

Shane

21

Sierra!

_____! You won't believe the news we got
EXCLAMATION

today! Shane Gray is going to be _____
VERB ENDING IN "ING"

at Camp Rock all summer. Remember how I told you that the

Connect _____ summer tour was canceled?
NUMBER

Ya know, 'cause Shane _____ during
VERB (PAST TENSE)

a video shoot when an assistant brought him a cup of

_____ instead of his usual _____
LIQUID   LIQUID

with _____? Well, now he is here!! I'm definitely
TYPE OF FOOD

going to try and take one of his _____.
PLURAL NOUN

I'll keep you posted!

Mitchie

Anybody Out There?

Hi Mom,

I tried to _____ you earlier but Cynthia said
         VERB

you were busy. So I thought I'd try _____
         VERB ENDING IN "ING"

instead. I hope the tour is going _____!
         ADVERB

Camp Rock is _____, as always. Ella and Peggy
         ADJECTIVE

are _____ in my bunk again, and we are
    VERB ENDING IN "ING"

so going to _____ Final Jam this year. Maybe
         VERB

you can come? I'll try to call you _____ again
         ADVERB

tomorrow.

Miss you,

Tess

Hi Campers!

Dear Mitchie and Connie,

I miss you _____ so much!
                    PLURAL NOUN

_____ is so quiet without the both of you,
     PLACE

and it's only been _____ days since you left
                          NUMBER

for Camp Rock. Mr. _____ next door came by
                     NAME OF CELEBRITY

today to tell me our maple tree is blocking his

_____. He's so _____! Connie,
     NOUN   SILLY WORD

can you send me your recipe for _____?
                                 TYPE OF FOOD (PLURAL)

I know you're busy, but I can't remember how to make

it. And I can't spend the summer without eating your

_____ food!
   ADJECTIVE

Love you guys,

Dad (aka Steve)

Stage Fright

Hi Dad,

There's an open mike tonight, and all the other

_____ will be there. Mom wants me to try
PLURAL NOUN

to _____ by myself, but I just can't do it.
VERB

The thought of all those eyes on me while I'm trying to

_____ is too much to handle. It's one thing
VERB

when I sing in the _____ by myself, but
PLACE

it's a whole other story to do it with _____
NUMBER

people listening—and watching! What if they don't

think I'm _____? Anyway, Mom says to tell
ADJECTIVE

you she'll send you her _____
TYPE OF FOOD (PLURAL)

recipe later.

Love,

Mitchie

Embracing Nature

N & J,

You have got to get me out of here! I'm not a little

_____! This _____
            NOUN   PLACE

was fun when we were _____ years old.
                                     NUMBER

But now it's way too _____ for my taste.
                             ADJECTIVE

I actually had to _____ in cold water!
                       VERB

I'm surrounded by _____ who are always
                       PLURAL NOUN

trying to _____ to me. Plus, my hair looks
               VERB

so _____ and my _____
     ADJECTIVE   NOUN

barely even gets reception out here. It's only got

_____ bars, and that's only if I stand on one
     NUMBER

foot and _____ while holding it. Save me!
              VERB

Later,

Shane

Burger Heaven*

Steve,

I can't leave you at home alone for even _____
NUMBER

days, can I? Here's the recipe:

I pound of ground _____
PLURAL NOUN

I cup of diced _____
PLURAL NOUN

I can of _____
LIQUID

A pinch of _____ and a dash of
NOUN

_____
TYPE OF FOOD

_____ well; then grill for about
VERB

_____ minutes per side.
NUMBER

Serve on warm, fluffy _____.
PLURAL NOUN

Enjoy! It'll be like I never left _____ at all.
PLACE

xoxo,

Connie

*Please note: These recipes are
for fill-in fun only. Do not try
to make them at home!

Overheard

N & J,

I heard something _____ today. I was hiding in
                     ADJECTIVE

the _____ to escape a pack of screaming
        PLURAL NOUN

girls—they're like wild _____, seriously. Anyway,
                          ANIMAL (PLURAL)

I was hiding and I overheard a girl _____
                                      VERB ENDING IN "ING"

inside the Music Mess Hall of Fame. She sounded like

_____ —no, even better than that. But when
FEMALE SINGER

I was finally able to _____ out of my hiding
                        VERB

spot, she was gone. I'll keep you posted. . . .

All alone in the woods,

Shane

More Than Just a Pretty Voice

Hi Sierra,

Last night I hung out with Caitlyn—that girl I met when I first arrived. She's really _____. She introduced

ADJECTIVE

me to another _____ named Lola. Lola

NOUN

_____ at the open mike night, and

VERB (PAST TENSE)

boy does that girl have _____! Her

PLURAL NOUN

_____ is a singer on Broadway. Caitlyn told

OCCUPATION

me that a lot of the _____ here don't care

PLURAL NOUN

about talent. She said everyone is focused on bling, which

is why Tess is the big _____ at camp. I've got

NOUN

a lot to learn. . . .

Miss you,

Mitchie

Liar, Liar

S,

I have officially lost my _____. I told everyone
                              NOUN

at _____, including Tess, that my mom is the
        PLACE

_____ of Hot Tunes in _____.
   OCCUPATION   COUNTRY

I know—what was I _____! It's just that Tess
                   VERB ENDING IN "ING"

and all the other _____ have parents that
                      PLURAL NOUN

do things like _____ for a living, instead of
                    VERB

cooking _____ for campers. I guess I just felt
             TYPE OF FOOD

_____ and I wanted to impress them all. What
    ADVERB

am I going to do now?!

Help!

M

Ella's Excitement

Dear Mom and Dad,

Tess had a _____ idea today. She invited this
                ADJECTIVE

like, _____ girl from _____ to
         ADJECTIVE   COUNTRY

bunk in our cabin. Whatev. She's so _____!
                                          ADJECTIVE

She has been in _____ music videos and
                     NUMBER

even knows _____. Fab! OMG, I have to
                CELEBRITY

_____ now. My lip gloss is _____
     VERB   VERB ENDING IN "ING"

and I have to reapply. My _____ are
                              PLURAL NOUN

so chapped.

Smooches,

Ella

In Deep

Dear Diary,

I have made such a mess. Now that Tess and her

_____ think my _____ is a
PLURAL NOUN   OCCUPATION

big wig at Hot Tunes in _____, they have asked
                              COUNTRY

me to _____ in their cabin for the summer. I'm
         VERB

psyched, but how am I going to keep it a secret that my

mom is really Connie of Connie's _____?
                                   VERB ENDING IN "ING"

Now I'll have to _____ out every morning at
                     VERB

like _____ to get to the kitchen and help my
        NUMBER

mom so no one finds out my _____.
                              NOUN

Ugh!

Mitchie

Shane Showed

Hi _____,

So, I gotta say, I was a little worried Shane might

_____ on me, but he's here! This morning I
VERB

had to dump cold _____ on him to get him
LIQUID

out of _____. But he just _____
PLACE   PLACE

over and went back to sleep. I think he's going to give me

a _____ all summer. Still, it's worth it to see
NOUN

Shane _____ again, just like he
VERB ENDING IN "ING"

used to before all this pop-star craziness. He really is a

_____ musician. I just have to remind him of
ADJECTIVE

that.

Rock on,

Brown

Mitchie's Moment

Dear Dad,

_____ , I did it! I actually _____
    SILLY WORD   VERB (PAST TENSE)

in front of a classroom full of _____
                                             PLURAL NOUN

today. Brown, the Camp _____ was our
                                  OCCUPATION

teacher, and he encouraged me to sing for him. So, I

_____ slunk up to the front. When I first
    ADVERB

started to _____, the class could barely hear
                 VERB

me. But then I felt _____ and I rocked it out.
                    ADVERB

I thought I sounded like a wounded _____,
                                  ANIMAL

but everyone said I was _____! Tess even
                          ADJECTIVE

asked me to _____ with her at Final Jam!
               VERB

_____!
    EXCLAMATION

Love,

Mitchie

34

Mr. Pop Star Himself!

Sierra,

Well, I finally met Shane Gray! Sort of. He

_____ into the kitchen! But I couldn't get
VERB (PAST TENSE)

caught working in there, so I quickly covered my face in

_____ to disguise myself! I can't have anyone,
TYPE OF FOOD

especially him, _____ that I'm the cook's
VERB ENDING IN "ING"

daughter. Anyway, Shane was a real _____.
NOUN

He complained about the_____ and said
TYPE OF FOOD (PLURAL)

he couldn't even go near his breakfast. He totally blamed

it on us! So, I set him straight. I told him he shouldn't talk

to _____ like that. When I become a famous
PLURAL NOUN

_____, I'll never change the way I treat
OCCUPATION

anybody—even the caterers!

Later,

Mitchie

Shane's First Class

Hey N & J,

Brown actually made me _____ a class today!
                              VERB

I told him that I wanted to speak to my _____ ,
                                          OCCUPATION

but he fed me some noise about staying true to

the _____ in my heart. Whatever! Anyway
         NOUN

the class wasn't so _____. I mean, there
                        ADJECTIVE

are a few students who have two left _____.
                                          NOUN

This one drummer could barely _____ , so I
                                    VERB

told him he just has to move the rhythm from

his _____ to his feet.
       PLURAL NOUN

Check ya,

Shane

Nearly Busted

Sierra,

This whole act is getting harder and harder to pull off.

At breakfast today, my mom came up to me when I was

_____ at a table with Tess and my other
VERB ENDING IN "ING"

new _____, Peggy and Ella. Mom asked
PLURAL NOUN

me how my _____ was! I totally had to cover by
TYPE OF FOOD

telling the other girls that my mom is a _____
ADJECTIVE

chef who has cooked for the likes of _____ and
CELEBRITY

_____ . I feel _____ about
CELEBRITY   ADVERB

lying, but I can't turn back now.

Gulp,

M

Eating with the Stars

Hi Mom and Dad,

OMG, this morning I totally ate the same eggs that

_____ has for _____ every
    CELEBRITY   NOUN

morning. The camp hired this new _____,
                                           OCCUPATION

or whatever they're called. The eggs looked like regular

_____, but I guess they were like, special or
TYPE OF FOOD (PLURAL)

something. I mean, if _____ ate them, they must
                                SAME CELEBRITY

be _____, right? They had _____
     ADJECTIVE   LIQUID

in them or maybe it was bits of _____.
                                     PLURAL NOUN

I don't know—I'm not a _____. But they
                              OCCUPATION

were dee-lish!

Love ya,

Ella

Campfire Jam

Hey again, Sierra,

Tonight I _____ onstage for the first time!
　　　　　VERB (PAST TENSE)

We had this thing called Campfire _____, and
　　　　　　　　　　　　　　　　SILLY WORD

Tess sang the lead _____ while Peggy,
　　　　　　　　　PLURAL NOUN

Ella, and I _____ backup. We dressed
　　　　　VERB (PAST TENSE)

up in silly _____ and wore our hair
　　　　TYPE OF CLOTHING (PLURAL)

in _____. And Shane Gray came! Tess
　　PLURAL NOUN

is _____ worried about impressing him, but
　　ADVERB

I'm over him after the scene in the kitchen. How's your

_____ going?
　NOUN

Hugs,

Mitchie

Who Is This?

Hey Mitchie,

What have you done with my _____ friend?
                          ADJECTIVE

_____ in the background while someone
VERB ENDING IN "ING"

else sings? That doesn't sound like the _____
                                        NOUN

I know. The Mitchie from _____ writes
                          COUNTRY

_____ songs. She doesn't fall prey to some
ADJECTIVE

queen _____ who steals the _____!
       ANIMAL   NOUN

Make sure you use your time at Camp Rock to live your

own _____, not someone else's. . . .
    PLURAL NOUN

Check back,

Sierra

Played

N & J,

That's it! I'm over this whole camp thing. Tonight I went to

this Campfire _____ and while I was watching
                  SILLY WORD

from a spot near the _____, I heard a couple
                          PLURAL NOUN

of _____ talking about me. Guess what
        PLURAL NOUN

they said? They said I was _____! They also said
                                ADJECTIVE

that Connect _____ is a _____
                    NUMBER   SILLY WORD

band. They even called us _____! I can't
                              PLURAL NOUN

believe people say such _____ things! Rescue
                            ADJECTIVE

me now, buds.

Out,

Shane

Tough It Out

Shane,

_____! You have got to get a grip,

EXCLAMATION

_____! We have gotten messages from you

NOUN

every day for like _____ days. We're starting

NUMBER

to wonder if maybe you want to come back to the sweet

life in _____ or something. And why are you

PLACE

always hiding in the _____? You're Shane

PLURAL NOUN

Gray! You wear _____ and play the

TYPE OF CLOTHING (PLURAL)

_____. You were on the cover of *Teen Talk*

INSTRUMENT

magazine _____ times last year! So tough it

NUMBER

out, and try to have a _____ time while you're

ADJECTIVE

at it.

Peace,

Nate

DIY Project

Shane,

So I was _____ yesterday, and
           VERB ENDING IN "ING"

I caught one of those DIY _____ on
                 PLURAL NOUN

TV. They showed a rockin' _____ print
               COLOR

for a _____ house—like the one you are
     ANIMAL

going to _____ for me at Camp Rock! It was
      VERB

_____ stories with a hot _____.
  NUMBER   NOUN

And the little _____ kitchen was off the
             ANIMAL

_____. _____ for entertaining
  NOUN   ADJECTIVE

the "chicks"! Get it?

Ha ha ha ha ha ha ha ha ha ha ha...

Jason

Beauty Sleep Needed

Hey _____,

You remember that _____ girl that I was kind
ADJECTIVE

enough to let _____ in my cabin? Well, she's
VERB

been _____ before the _____
VERB ENDING IN "ING"   NOUN

comes up every morning. Isn't that strange? Where is

she _____ at that hour? She was also really
VERB ENDNG IN "ING"

_____ about this _____ she writes
ADJECTIVE   NOUN

in all the time. She's hiding something, and I'm going to

find out what it is . . . .

Still snooping,

Tess

Red Hot Chili*

Hi Sweetheart!

Here is that chili recipe your mom wanted.

10 pounds of cubed _____
INSTRUMENT

5 pounds of diced _____
PLURAL NOUN

2 heads of minced _____
NOUN

Saute until _____.
COLOR

Then add:

10 _____ of chicken stock
PLURAL NOUN

10 tablespoons of cumin from _____
COUNTRY

10 teaspoons of _____
LIQUID

_____ everything together and let the
VERB

pot _____ for at least _____
VERB   NUMBER

hours.

Love you both,

Dad

*Please note: These recipes are for fill-in fun only. Do not try to make them at home!

Food Fight

Hi Mom,

How's Broadway? I bet _____ is super hot in
                              CITY
the summer. Things are heating up here, too! Today there

was a massive food fight in the _____. By the
                                        PLACE
end, _____ and _____
      TYPE OF FOOD (PLURAL)   LIQUID

were everywhere! It all started when this one girl,

_____ , accidently tripped Tess Tyler
NAME OF FEMALE IN ROOM

(I've told you about her—and her temper!). Tess thought it

was intentional and before you knew it, _____
                                                NOUN

ensued. It was total mess-hall madness!

Reporting live from _____,
                          PLACE

Lola

Risky Business

Hey Sierra,

Get this: there was a _____ fight in
                          NOUN

_____ yesterday! My friend Caitlyn
          PLACE

took the fall for the whole thing, and Brown assigned

her _____ duty as punishment! (That's sort of
        PLACE

funny since I've been working in _____ all
                                    SAME PLACE

summer and I don't think of it as _____!) This is a
                                      NOUN

total _____, Sierra! I just worry Caitlyn's
          NOUN

going to find out my secret and tell all the other

_____ at Camp Rock! The worst part is,
        PLURAL NOUN

it's all my fault that she's in trouble.

Sad,

M

It's On

Hi Mom and Dad,

Tess and I had a _____ disagreement today.
ADJECTIVE

She apparently doesn't like the _____
TYPE OF FOOD

that landed on her Gucci shoes—whatev. She also said

she's going to have her _____ sue
OCCUPATION

me. She walks around Camp Rock like she owns the

place. All because her mom has _____
VERB (PAST TENSE)

a few _____. I mean, like that's so
PLURAL NOUN

_____? She thinks I'm jealous of her, but that
ADJECTIVE

couldn't be further from the _____.
NOUN

Love you,

Caitlyn

Tess Tries Again

Hi there, Mom,

I tried calling you again _____. I spoke to
                            ADVERB

Cynthia at _____, but she said you were
                PLACE

_____ at the _____. Did
VERB ENDING IN "ING"   NOUN

she give you the message? I wanted to tell you that camp is

_____ this summer. Maybe you can try calling
     ADJECTIVE

me on my _____ soon and I can tell you all
                NOUN

about it. A lot has happened. Okay, I love you, Mom. Hope

the _____ album is going _____.
        ADJECTIVE   ADVERB

Your daughter,

Tess

New Song

Hey guys,

I was tooling around with some new lyrics for a Connect

_____ song. Tell me what you think:
NUMBER

I'm _____ free.
    VERB ENDING IN "ING"

Chasing down my _____.
                 PLURAL NOUN

Can't you _____.
          VERB

Can't you _____.
          VERB

Tired of feeling _____.
                 ADVERB

_____ every day!
VERB ENDING IN "ING"

Dig it,

Shane

P.S. I met a _____ here. She's really down to
             NOUN

_____ and she's making me feel cool about
NOUN

writing new kinds of _____.
                     PLURAL NOUN

Kitchen Help

Hi Steve,

Things are going _____ at camp. The
                        ADJECTIVE

_____ was a hit! There's a lovely young
   TYPE OF FOOD

_____ that's been assigned to help me in
       NOUN

the kitchen. Her name is Caitlyn and she helped me chop

_____ for _____ night. She
   PLURAL NOUN   TYPE OF FOOD

seems like the kind of girl that Mitchie would be friends

with back at _____. But Mitchie has made
                    PLACE

friends with some _____ girls this summer.
                          ADJECTIVE

I worry about her, Steve . . . .

Love to you!

Connie

Busted!

Sierra,

Well, I should have expected this. Caitlyn knows that my mom is the cook here, and not the _____ at

OCCUPATION

Hot Tunes in _____. She found out when I tried

COUNTRY

to sneak out of the kitchen and tripped on a bucketful of

_____. I spilled _____ everywhere!

LIQUID   TYPE OF FOOD

Talk about _____! I'm sure she's going to

ADJECTIVE

_____, and then the whole camp will know I'm

VERB

nothing but a _____. Looks like I won't be able

NOUN

to show my face around Camp Rock for much longer.

Boo-hoo,

Mitchie

Overseas Adventure

Hi Daddy,

Can I have some _____ to go to
$\qquad$ PLURAL NOUN

_____ after Camp Rock is over?
$\qquad$ COUNTRY

Pretty please? This _____ at camp named
$\qquad$ NOUN

Mitchie is really _____. She even writes her
$\qquad$ ADJECTIVE

own _____ and everything. Anyway, her
$\qquad$ PLURAL NOUN

mom is the _____ in _____ or
$\qquad$ OCCUPATION $\qquad$ PLACE

_____ or somewhere. I totally want to take a
$\qquad$ COUNTRY

trip there.

Thanks, Daddy!

Ella

Old Tricks

Hey _____,
PERSON IN ROOM

Guess who is up to her old _____
PLURAL NOUN

again? That's right—Tess Tyler! Tonight, while I was

_____ at the _____
VERB ENDING IN "ING"   ARTICLE OF CLOTHING

Jam, she screamed, "_____!". The entire
ANIMAL

room turned to _____ instead of watching
VERB

me. All because she can't stand when she's not in the

_____! But Mitchie stood up for me. She
NOUN

might be _____ than I thought . . .
ADJECTIVE

TTYL,

Caitlyn

Note to Self

Dear _____,
PERSON IN ROOM

I've been writing _____ lyrics recently.
ADJECTIVE

Probably because of all the _____ — or maybe
NOUN

because of _____. Here are some:
PERSON IN ROOM

Some say I'm _____.
ADJECTIVE

Some call me a _____.
NOUN

But, I take their _____,
PLURAL NOUN

And I wish them _____.
ADVERB

I'm _____ to breathe.
VERB ENDING IN "ING"

I'm not _____ away.
VERB ENDING IN "ING"

Thoughts?

Mitchie

Pajama Jam

Hola _____!

Last night I went to Pajama _____ here at

Camp Rock, and it was wild! The _____ sang

songs that were outta this _____. But the best

part were the even wilder pjs that everyone

_____ in. One girl wore a _____!

And three girls wore _____ shorts with a

white _____. I wore my signature

pair of _____—always in style!

Catch you,

Andy

Checking In

Shane,

I just wanted to tell you that the song you sent is

_____! It's _____ school Shane,
    ADJECTIVE   ADJECTIVE

in a good way! It reminds me of the stuff we used to write

when we were _____ at Camp Rock just
                   PLURAL NOUN

a few _____ ago. I know it feels like an
        PLURAL NOUN

eternity since we were those guys, but hang on to that

part of yourself. I'm starting to think it's a better

_____ than what the label is making us do.
    NOUN

_____ on that idea while you finish building
    VERB

my _____ house!
    ANIMAL

Later man,

Jason

P.S.???

Shane,

What is up with that _____ P.S. you tacked
                          ADJECTIVE

on the end of your last message? You can't drop a

_____ like that and not explain more!
     NOUN

C'mon, man, I'm your _____— you can share!
                          NOUN

What's the _____'s name anyway? Is she
                NOUN

_____? And most importantly, do you think she
   ADJECTIVE

can _____ with the big _____,
         VERB   PLURAL NOUN

or what? I fully expect an intro when we _____
                                              VERB

up for Final _____, got it?
              TYPE OF FOOD

Later,

Nate

Lip-Gloss Emergency

Dear Mom,

Can you please send more lip gloss _____?
                                        ADVERB

I'm almost out of it in _____. Can you also
                              COLOR

_____ that one I like called _____
        VERB   SILLY WORD

by _____? If my lips aren't _____,
      CELEBRITY   ADJECTIVE

I will so _____. I'm not even kidding. It's a
                 VERB

total emergency!

Hope you can help!

Ella

P.S. I'm also running low on pink _____ and
                                        NOUN

my _____ are beginning to chip!!
        PLURAL NOUN

Lightbulb

Hey N & J,

I figured out a way to make _____ with
VERB ENDING IN "ING"

the winner of Camp Rock's Final Jam _____.
ADJECTIVE

I have got to find the girl with the _____
NOUN

from the _____ and get her in the Jam. She
PLACE

could totally _____! To make it happen, I
VERB

might have, sort of, put the _____ out to
NOUN

the other _____. I know it sounds like a
PLURAL NOUN

_____ plan, but I think it could work! Keep
ADJECTIVE

your _____ crossed. This could be the
PLURAL NOUN

beginning of something _____.
SILLY WORD

Shane

New Moves

Hey ____________________,
PERSON IN ROOM

Just saying hey from ________________________.
PLACE

The ____________________ star Shane Gray is a guest
SILLY WORD

instructor this summer. Turns out, that ________________
NOUN

has got some serious moves! He helped me improve my

____________________ so I can ________________
PLURAL NOUN VERB

like he and his boys do on stage. I'm gonna surprise the

____________________ at Final Jam. *And* he just asked
PLURAL NOUN

me to help him with something really ________________. I
ADJECTIVE

can't tell you what it is yet, but you'll find out soon enough.

Its ________________!
EXCLAMATION

Be talking to you,

Andy

The Search Begins

Dear _____,
PERSON IN ROOM

I heard that Shane _____ is looking for a certain
COLOR

_____ with a magical voice that he heard once.
NOUN

_____! He wants to _____ with
EXCLAMATION   VERB

"the voice" on his next album. It's got to be me! After all,

you taught me how the singers on _____
PLACE

project their voices. I'm going to find that

_____ star and show him what I've got. Wish
ADJECTIVE

me luck becoming Mrs. Shane _____. I mean,
COLOR

wish me luck _____ with him. Ha!
VERB ENDING IN "ING"

TTYL,

Lola

This Just In

Dear _____-in-Chief,
        OCCUPATION

I thought you might be interested to hear some news

about Shane Gray for your next issue of _____
                                            NOUN

Scoop magazine. By the way, your mag rocks! Anyway,

Shane is at _____ this summer, which
                  PLACE

everyone knows. But what they *don't* know is that he is

_____ all over the place with one mission:
VERB ENDING IN "ING"

to find some _____ he heard sing once. He's
              NOUN

asked every _____ here to help him find her!
           NOUN

On the lookout,

Anonymous

Pretty, Shiny Things

Hi Sierra,

Even though I've been at Camp Rock for nearly _____

NUMBER

days, I'm still surprised by how spoiled some of the

campers are. Like, Tess, for example. She has this charm

bracelet that her _____ gave her. Every time

OCCUPATION

T.J. Tyler wins a _____, Tess gets another

NOUN

charm. I wouldn't be surprised if it's from that fancy store

on Rodeo _____ called _____.

VERB   SILLY WORD

What if my _____ were like that, and I could

PLURAL NOUN

have anything I wanted? No more helping Mom cook

_____ for _____ hungry

TYPE OF FOOD (PLURAL)   NUMBER

campers, that's for sure.

Woe is me,

Mitchie

So Over It

Hey Mom,

You wouldn't believe all the drama here this week! Shane

Gray is on a mission to find some _____ he
                                          NOUN

heard _____. Now, every _____
              VERB   NOUN

at camp is _____ all over him, trying to
              VERB ENDING IN "ING"

be chosen. Why is everyone so _____ to be
                                      ADJECTIVE

attached to a _____? Whatev, it's no
                      NOUN

biggie. Send me more gummy _____
                                TYPE OF ANIMAL (PLURAL)

soon, okay? Thanks!

Caitlyn

Secret Meeting

Hi Peggy,

I know you're here at _____ with me, but
                        PLACE

Tess was all _____ about this, so shhhhh! I'm
              ADJECTIVE

going to _____ for Shane Gray to see if my
          VERB

_____ is the one he's been looking for. I want
    NOUN

to make him a _____, but I don't know how
                  NOUN

to _____ with my computer. Actually, I've
    VERB

never used it. So, can you meet me at _____
                                        PLACE

tomorrow to show me? Remember, _____ is the
                                 SILLY WORD

word—shhh!

E.L.I. (That's my code _____, but it's really me,
                          NOUN

Ella!)

No Glass Slipper

Nate and Jason,

Well, my plan was a _____ one. Every
                            ADJECTIVE

_____ at camp showed up to _____
      NOUN   VERB

for me, but I haven't found the voice yet. It's like I have a

glass _____ and that girl is the only one it fits.
       TYPE OF SHOE

But the other _____ here are not afraid to
                  PLURAL NOUN

try. One sang to me when I was trying to _____!
                                                VERB

Can't a guy get some privacy? And _____ of
                                          NUMBER

them even tracked me down to the _____!
                                        PLACE

The search continues....

Shane

Mission: Impossible

Dear E.L.I.,

You could have just talked to me when Tess was not around.

You didn't have to send a _____ through the

<u>NOUN</u>

US Mail! I will def help you make a _____ for

<u>NOUN</u>

Shane _____. And don't worry, I won't tell

<u>COLOR</u>

Tess about your _____ scheme. Love your code

<u>ADJECTIVE</u>

name by the way! I think mine will be _____.

<u>CELEBRITY (FEMALE)</u>

I feel like we're _____ in a secret group!

<u>PLURAL NOUN</u>

It's like CRSI—Camp Rock Secret Intelligence! See you in our

cabin!

Talk to you soon,

_____

<u>SAME CELEBRITY (FEMALE)</u>

Lost in Translation

Dear Peggy,

Something weird is going on. I just got a _____
NOUN

from a famous celebrity! How does she know I'm at Camp

Rock? Do you _____ what's going on? Should
VERB

I tell Brown? _____ ! I need your help!
SILLY WORD

Ella

P.S. Did you get my _____ I sent? I think it
NOUN

might have gotten _____ in the mail!
VERB (PAST TENSE)

To Make It Simple

Ella,

Meet me at the _____ behind _____
                        NOUN   PLACE

at _____ o'clock tonight. Bring your
        NUMBER

_____ and I'll show you how to use it. Be sure
        NOUN

to _____ carefully so you don't wake up the
        VERB

other _____. They go to bed at
            PLURAL NOUN

_____ o'clock.
        NUMBER

Your friend and bunk mate,

Peggy

P.S. I was the one who wrote you and said my name

was _____.
        CELEBRITY (FEMALE)

Boating Trip

Hi Sierra,

I was _____ near the lake today, when
VERB ENDING IN "ING"

I heard Shane _____ singing. When he saw
COLOR

me, he asked me to join him. Before I knew it, we were

_____ together in a _____
VERB ENDING IN "ING"   NOUN

on the lake. He's not the most talented _____
                                                    NOUN

—we _____ in circles—but he is a really good
VERB (PAST TENSE)

_____. He's a cool guy. I mean, I like him for his
OCCUPATION

musical _____—that's all! Still, I wonder
PLURAL NOUN

what he _____ of me?
VERB (PAST TENSE)

Miss you,

M

I Knew It!

Hey _____,
       PERSON IN ROOM

I told you that _____ girl Mitchie was
                    ADJECTIVE

up to something! I can smell a _____ a
                                    ANIMAL

mile away. It's a gift. Anyway, I was totally right! I

keep _____ her hanging out with
        VERB ENDING IN "ING"

Shane _____! Doesn't she know that I have dibs
         COLOR

on all _____ pop stars? It's just the way
          ADJECTIVE

it goes. I knew Mitchie was trouble from the second she

set foot at _____.
                 PLACE

Freaking out,

Tess

New Calling?

Hi _____,

I'm still on _____ duty here at Camp

Rock. I cannot believe I got in trouble over spilled

_____, but whatev. Connie Torres is really

_____, and she's a great _____!

She's showing me how to make _____

with _____ on top! Maybe if the whole

music industry thing doesn't work out for me, I can

_____ at culinary school instead!

Love always,

Caitlyn

Connect Three

Daddy!

_____! _____! All _____
    EXCLAMATION   EXCLAMATION   NUMBER

of the members of Connect _____ showed up at
                                NUMBER

camp today! They sang a new song and it was amazing! I

think I'm going to _____ right here and now.
                   VERB

It's been _____ having Shane here all summer,
        ADJECTIVE

but now Nate and Jason, too?! It's too _____
                                 ADJECTIVE

to be true, right?! OMG, I think I might _____
                                 VERB

out!

Love you,

Ella

Capture the Flag

Dear Parental Units,

Just wanted to check in. We played capture the

_____ today. It was a _____
    NOUN   ADJECTIVE

game! I was on the _____ team, but
                            COLOR

Barron was on the _____ team. My team
                          ANIMAL

was _____ at first, but we made a
      VERB ENDING IN "ING"

huge comeback because of yours truly. I hid behind a

_____ for a while, then I _____
    NOUN   ADVERB

leaped out and captured their _____!
                                       NOUN

Talk to you later,

Sander

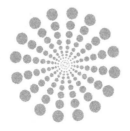

Caught Red-Handed

Bonjour Mademoiselle,

Guess what? I was totally right— yet again! I was

_____ near the _____ at Camp
VERB ENDING IN "ING"   PLACE

Rock today, and I heard Mitchie talking to

_____. It turns out that Mitchie's
PERSON IN ROOM

mother is actually the camp _____! How
                                OCCUPATION

_____ is that? Now, I just have to find the
ADJECTIVE

_____ moment to drop this _____
ADJECTIVE   NOUN

on everyone else. Mitchie's _____ minutes are
                                NUMBER

so over.

Ta-ta for now,

Tess

Pants on Fire

Sierra,

Liar, liar, my _____ are on fire.

ARTICLE OF CLOTHING (PLURAL)

And now, everyone knows it. Tess outed me in front of

everyone at Camp _____, including my mom!

NOUN

I've never seen my mom look at me the way she did! It

was _____! Even Shane _____ and

ADJECTIVE   VERB (PAST TENSE)

he looked so mad! I've never felt more _____ in

ADVERB

my life. I want to come home _____!

ADVERB

Miss you,

Mitchie

Status Report

Dear _____ Records dudes,
COLOR

Per your _____, I am writing to inform you
NOUN

that Shane Gray is progressing _____
ADVERB

during his time at my camp: Camp Rock. He's been

_____ with the other campers,
VERB ENDING IN "ING"

writing new _____, and generally
PLURAL NOUN

learning to be _____. I think you'll
ADJECTIVE

be pleased with his improved attitude, and should

have no reason to cancel his _____
VERB ENDING IN "ING"

contract.

Thank you,

Brown Cesario

_____, Camp Rock
OCCUPATION

The Fibber

Hi Honey,

This summer has been full of surprises. And our

_____ daughter is the biggest one of all! I
ADJECTIVE

found out today that Mitchie has been telling the campers

that I work in _____, as a _____!
PLACE   OCCUPATION

It seems she was trying to impress the other campers. But I

don't get it—I thought being a chef was _____.
ADJECTIVE

What about those famous ones on television, like Mario

_____ and the Barefoot _____?
SILLY WORD   EXCLAMATION

I just don't understand her sometimes, Steve, I really don't.

Confused,

Connie

Musical Memories

Dear _____,

I was thinking about you the other day. I'm still working at

_____ and one of the _____

sounds just like you. Remember that time back in the day

when we toured with _____? We went from

_____ all the way to _____!

How many _____ do you think we saw —

maybe _____ in just one summer? Those were

_____ times, my friend.

Peace,

Brown

Songwriting Workshop

Hey guys,

I'm still _____ at you—sort of. But I did
        ADJECTIVE

something kind of cool today. I led a workshop. I

had the _____ all write a song in
          PLURAL NOUN

_____ minutes. I made them do it
        NUMBER

_____ to show them that they shouldn't over
      ADVERB

_____ it. It worked! Some of them wrote
      VERB

about _____ things like _____,
        ADJECTIVE   PLURAL NOUN

and some wrote about _____. Still, I was
                        TYPES OF FOOD

pretty impressed.

Later,

Shane

Tess's Song

Hi Mom,

Today, Shane _____ taught a songwriting
                    COLOR

_____. I wrote these _____.
       NOUN   PLURAL NOUN

What do you think?

    I woke up _____.
                 ADVERB

    And realized something _____.
                              ADJECTIVE

    I wanna _____.
             VERB

    I wanna _____.
             VERB

That's all I have so far, but Shane said it was _____.
                                                    ADJECTIVE

I'm sure Mitchie couldn't write lyrics this _____!
                                                ADJECTIVE

Call me _____, if you have time.
              ADVERB

Love,

Tess

If I Were A Rock Star

Dear _____,
<small>PERSON IN ROOM</small>

I was thinking today that if I'm going to be a

_____, I need to start planning! So if I were a
<small>NOUN</small>

_____, I'd have _____ and
<small>NOUN</small>   <small>TYPE OF FOOD</small>

_____ in my dressing _____.
<small>LIQUID</small>   <small>PLACE</small>

If I were a rock star, I'd have _____ people
<small>NUMBER</small>

_____ for me—just 'cause I could. If I were
<small>VERB ENDING IN "ING"</small>

a rock star, I'd hire a _____ to do things
<small>OCCUPATION</small>

like massage my feet and feed my _____. But
<small>ANIMAL</small>

don't worry, no matter how _____ I get, I'll
<small>ADJECTIVE</small>

never forget you!

Dreaming big,

Peggy

The Pariah of Camp Rock

Sierra, Sierra, Sierra,

I am a total social _____ now. When I walked
                        NOUN

into my _____ class, everyone looked at
        VERB ENDING IN "ING"

me like I had _____ heads. I went and sat
                NUMBER

in the corner with my _____ down. They
                        NOUN

all _____ I'm a liar because Tess
        VERB

_____ me out. It's so _____!
VERB (PAST TENSE)   ADJECTIVE

_____ wouldn't even look at me. How am I
CELEBRITY

going to get myself out of this mess?

Hopeless in the _____,
                PLURAL NOUN

Mitchie

84

Water Fight

Hiya!

It's just me reporting _____ from Camp Rock.
ADVERB

Today, there was a water fight after _____ class. It
NOUN

started when Brown squirted Dee with a _____.
NOUN

Then Dee got him back by pouring a _____ full
NOUN

of water over his head. After that, every _____
NOUN

in the _____ joined in, and before I knew it,
PLACE

I was drenched. Felt _____ though. It was
ADJECTIVE

_____ degrees outside today!
NUMBER

Catch you later,

Andy

Fessing Up

Hey Dad,

I guess by now Mom has told you what I did. You must

be _____. So I just wanted to say I'm
   VERB ENDING IN "ING"

_____. I never meant to hurt Mom—or you—
   SILLY WORD

or anyone. I just wanted to know what it feels like to have

_____, Dad. I just wanted to experience
   PLURAL NOUN

being one of the _____ girls. I know I messed
              ADJECTIVE

up. Guess I got what was coming to me, though, huh?

Hope you aren't too _____,
                   ADJECTIVE

Mitchie

Lola's Letter

Hi!

Guess what? I think I'm going to _____ with
                                        VERB

my _____ Barron and Sander at this year's
        PLURAL NOUN

Final Jam! You're going to _____ up here to
                                    VERB

watch, right? It's going to be _____, so you have
                                        ADJECTIVE

to be there! We've been practicing like crazy to make

our performance _____. I am going to
                        ADJECTIVE

_____ around the stage, while Barron and
        VERB

Sander _____ together. The Final _____
                VERB   TYPE OF FOOD

award will be ours!

Yay!

Lola

Unexpected Twist

Hey buds,

Just when I though I'd met a _____ I could
                                          NOUN

trust—one that liked me for me, not because I can get

_____ stuff and get into places like The
      ADJECTIVE

_____ Lounge—I find out that I was completely
      COUNTRY

wrong! She was _____ all summer—to my
                    VERB ENDING IN "ING"

face—to all the _____ faces, actually. I
                      PLURAL NOUN

never expected to feel this _____, but I really
                                    ADVERB

do.

Bummed,

Shane

More to Mitchie

Hi _____,
NAME OF PERSON IN ROOM

So you know how I _____ you about
VERB (PAST TENSE)

Mitchie? How she completely _____ for Tess's
VERB (PAST TENSE)

games? Well, after Tess acted like the _____
NOUN

she is, Mitchie woke up. She totally called Tess out

on being so _____. Now we are good
ADJECTIVE

_____ and we are even going to
PLURAL NOUN

_____ together at Final Jam. _____!
VERB   EXCLAMATION

I should have _____ there was more to
VERB (PAST TENSE)

Mitchie.

Rock on,

Caitlyn

True Friend

Hey Sierra,

Me again! Camp Rock has taught me about many different

_____. But one thing I didn't expect to
PLURAL NOUN

learn was the meaning of _____ friendship.
ADJECTIVE

Even after the whole _____ mess,
VERB ENDING IN "ING"

Caitlyn is still by my side. So are Barron, Sander, and

Lola—even after I _____ ignored their attempts
ADVERB

to be nice to me at the beginning of camp! I'm so

lucky to count you as a _____, too. See you
NOUN

soon, okay?

M

Regime Change?

Dear Mom,

Tess is starting to drive me really _____! I'm
<small>ADJECTIVE</small>

tired of being in her _____ all the time. I need
<small>NOUN</small>

to be in the _____ for a change. How are things
<small>NOUN</small>

at _____? I can't wait to come home and
<small>PLACE</small>

have my favorite _____. But before that,
<small>TYPE OF FOOD (PLURAL)</small>

I have to get through Final Jam—with Tess. _____!
<small>SILLY WORD</small>

For once, I wish I could be the _____!
<small>NOUN</small>

Wish me luck!

Peggy

Speaking Up

Sierra,

I finally got the _____ to stand up
NOUN

to Tess! It happened in _____. She was
PLACE

acting like a spoiled _____, and in front of
NOUN

everyone, she _____ me to tell my mom the
VERB (PAST TENSE)

_____ was dry! She is so _____!
ANIMAL   ADJECTIVE

So, I said, "_____, Tess." I thought it was time
SILLY WORD

for her to have a dose of her own _____. Tess
NOUN

acted like she didn't care, but I know deep down, she felt

_____. About time, right?!
ADVERB

Props for me!

Mitchie

Final Jam Duties

Attention _____!
PLURAL NOUN

The following is a list of duties that must be performed in

order for Final Jam to be successful:

Paint the _____: Barron and Sander
PLACE

Hang the _____ above the stage: Andy
NOUN

Make a sign that says _____: Tess and Ella
EXCLAMATION

Clean out the _____: Peggy
PLACE

That's all for now! I'll post another _____ with
NOUN

new _____ tomorrow.
PLURAL NOUN

Rock on,

Camp _____ Brown
OCCUPATION

Looking Up

Hi Dad!

Things are _____ up here at Camp
_____VERB ENDING IN "ING"_____

Rock. I am going to _____ at Final Jam with
_____VERB_____

Caitlyn. Yesterday, we picked out our _____
_____ADJECTIVE

costumes. We are going to wear _____
_____COLOR

hats with a _____. Caitlyn is
____ARTICLE OF CLOTHING

going to _____ like _____ at
____VERB____ ____CELEBRITY

last year's _____ Music Awards. I'm still
____COUNTRY

_____ about giving a performance in front of
____ADVERB

_____ campers and parents and stuff. But I
____NUMBER

think it's a _____ in the right direction!
____NOUN

Love,

Mitchie

If I Toured the World

Hey man,

I was thinking that when I'm a famous rock _____,
NOUN

I'm going to tour the _____. I'll get to
NOUN

travel to _____ and _____.
PLACE   COUNTRY

I'll finally have a chance to visit the _____
ADJECTIVE

Wall of _____, _____ in
COUNTRY   VERB

the _____ Canyon, and see the bright
ADJECTIVE

lights of _____. Now, all I have to do is
PLACE

_____ at Final Jam, and I'll be well on my
VERB

way!

Outtie,

Sander

Mitchie the Thief

Hi Sierra,

Well, not only is your friend Mitchie a liar, but apparently

now I'm a _____, too! Tess might be the most
         OCCUPATION

_____ person in the world. She framed Caitlyn
    ADJECTIVE

and I! She _____ her _____
          VERB (PAST TENSE)   ARTICLE OF CLOTHING

under the _____ in the kitchen. Then, she
          PLURAL NOUN

told Brown that we had _____ it! When
                       VERB (PAST TENSE)

he came to investigate, there it was (right where I'm

sure she _____ it), so we looked like the
         VERB (PAST TENSE)

_____ parties.
    ADJECTIVE

Framed,

Mitchie

Our Troublemaker

Dear Steve,

I don't know what has gotten into Mitchie! After she

_____ and got _____ ,
VERB (PAST TENSE)   VERB (PAST TENSE)

I thought she'd lay low for the rest of the summer. But

today Brown barged into the _____ with
                                         PLACE

Tess Tyler. Tess claims Mitchie and Caitlyn stole her

_____! I have a _____
ARTICLE OF CLOTHING   ADJECTIVE

time believing that Mitchie did it. But with no

_____ to the contrary, Mitchie is no longer
NOUN

allowed to _____ at Final Jam. I feel so awful!
                    VERB

Wish you were here,

Connie

Next Stop, Broadway

Hi Mom!

Final Jam is just a few _____ away and I'm getting
                          PLURAL NOUN

_____ ! I bet this is how you _____
   ADJECTIVE   VERB

right before your _____ opens on Broadway.
                       NOUN

Even though I'm _____ , I _____
                     ADJECTIVE   VERB

the buzz and excitement around _____ . It
                                      PLACE

makes me _____ that maybe Broadway is where
              VERB

I want to be. But I shouldn't count my _____
                                        ANIMAL (PLURAL)

before they are _____ . First, I need to win
                 VERB (PAST TENSE)

Final Jam!

Your aspiring star,

Lola

Serious Brown

Oh, _____,
PERSON IN ROOM

Today was rough, mate. I had to tell _____
NUMBER

campers that they are not allowed to _____
VERB

at Final Jam. It's their punishment for taking another

camper's _____— even though I
ARTICLE OF CLOTHING

really don't think they would do something like that. I just

don't understand _____ today. When we
PLURAL NOUN

rocked it was pure—all about the _____. Not
NOUN

anymore! Now it's all about winning—no matter what the

cost.

Uncool,

_____
COLOR

One More Try

Hi Mom,

I haven't heard from you in a while, and I just wanted to remind you that Final Jam is coming up _____.
ADVERB

I am doing a routine similar to the one you did at the _____ award show. The one where
YEAR

you _____ across the stage with
VERB (PAST TENSE)

_____ spotlights flashing. Anyway, I spoke to
COLOR

your assistant, _____, again today. Hope you
CELEBRITY

can get here in time for the Final Jam. I got that

_____ girl Mitchie out of the way—
ADJECTIVE

_____.
EXCLAMATION

Lots of love,

Your Tess

Oops, I Didn't Do It Again

Dear Dad,

Okay, let me just say that even though I did

_____ and tell the other campers that Mom
    VERB

worked in _____ and all, I am *not* a thief! Dad,
    COUNTRY

Tess totally set Caitlyn and me up to _____ us
    VERB

out of her way so that she can win Final Jam. She used to be

one of Caitlyn's _____, and then she was
    PLURAL NOUN

one of mine. But now we both _____ what she
    VERB

is really like—and it is not nice. I know you'll be here to see

Final Jam, but I won't be one of the campers who gets to

_____.
    VERB

Sadly,

Mitchie

Dressing the Part

Hi _____,
   PLURAL NOUN

OMG! Tess and Peggy and I have like, _____
                                        ADJECTIVE

costumes for Final Jam. They are _____ and
                                       COLOR

covered in sparkly _____. They make us
                        PLURAL NOUN

look like pretty little _____ swimming in
                             PLURAL NOUN

the _____ or something. Thanks for sending
        NOUN

all those extra _____! I think my lips are
                     PLURAL NOUN

going to have to be extraglossy to match my outfit!

Yay!

Ella

Inquiring Minds

Hey man,

Inquiring _____ want to know: have you
        PLURAL NOUN

found the girl with the _____ yet or what?
        NOUN

We are starting to think perhaps she is a figment of your

_____, dude. You better _____
  NOUN   VERB

quickly if you're going to find in her in time for Final

_____. T-minus _____ days
  TYPE OF FOOD   NUMBER

and counting . . .

Later,

Nate and Jason

P.S. Dude! We'll be up there to _____ the jam.
                  VERB

You better have finished my _____!
             OBJECT IN ROOM

Help a Bandmate Out!

Hey dudes,

You are _____ soon, right? I need
VERB ENDING IN "ING"

your _____! Brown told me we are going
VERB

to be the judges for Final Jam. That's some

_____ pressure. And no, I haven't found
ADVERB

the voice _____! It's like looking for a
EXCLAMATION

_____ in a haystack! Maybe with you
NOUN

_____ here, I'll have more luck.
NUMBER

See you soon,

Shane

P.S. Jason—one more _____ about the
NOUN

_____ and the band will need to be renamed
NOUN

Connect Two!

Final Call

Sierra,

I am one smart _____! I realized that
                    TYPE OF FOOD

Brown specifically told Caitlyn and me that we were banned

from competing until *"the end of Final Jam"*. So, the second

the curtain _____, we made our move. And
              VERB (PAST TENSE)

I did it! I _____ in front of everyone! And as I
              VERB

was _____, Shane came on the
      VERB ENDING IN "ING"

_____ and started _____
      NOUN   VERB ENDING IN "ING"

with me! I felt like I was in a _____. Turns out /
                                  NOUN

was the voice he had been looking for! Oh, S, I have had some

ups and _____ here at Camp Rock, but
          PLURAL NOUN

tonight was definitely the high point.

Ahhh!

Mitchie

I'm On My Way

Mom!!!

_____! _____! _____!
EXCLAMATION   EXCLAMATION   EXCLAMATION

I _____ Final Jam! This has been the
   VERB (PAST TENSE)

absolute best _____ of my life. I stood up to
                    NOUN

Tess and _____ on my own. Now I get a
            VERB (PAST TENSE)

chance to _____ with Shane Gray—on a record!!
              VERB

_____! I guess _____ really do
SILLY WORD   PLURAL NOUN

come true!

Soon to be a _____,
                  NOUN

Peggy (aka Margaret Dupree—get used to seeing that name

in _____!)
   PLURAL NOUN

Great News!

Dear Cynthia,

Thank you for making sure my mom came up for Final Jam.

I was so _____ to see her. At first I thought she
        ADJECTIVE

wasn't listening. She kept talking on her _____.
                                     NOUN

But she _____ me I get to come on
       VERB (PAST TENSE)

_____ with her! I never _____
  NOUN   VERB (PAST TENSE)

that coming! So I didn't win Final Jam—hanging out with

my mom is even _____!
              ADJECTIVE

Thanks!

Tess

Believe It!

Hey _____,

Well, this year's Final Jam was one for the

_____. Not only did Mitchie and I end
PLURAL NOUN

up doing a _____ song at the end, Peggy—I
ADJECTIVE

guess I should say Margaret Dupree—won! And, just

when I thought things couldn't get _____,
ADJECTIVE

Tess Tyler actually said she was sorry! Can you believe

that? I thought _____ would fly over the
ANIMAL (PLURAL)

_____ before she would apologize. It sure was
NOUN

a wild _____!
NOUN

See you soon,

Caitlyn

108

Job Well Done

Dear Mr. Gray,

After getting several _____ from
                        PLURAL NOUN

Camp Director Brown regarding your progress, we

are _____ to tell you that Connect
      ADJECTIVE

_____'s tour can resume. Your commitment
   NUMBER

to _____ and the _____
      PLACE   PLURAL NOUN

shows us that you are as committed to your

_____. We are excited to _____
      NOUN   VERB

your new song and the recording you will do with

whomever wins Final Jam.

Regards,

_____
   CELEBRITY

President of A & R

_____ Records
   COLOR

Breaking News

Dear _____ Scoop readers,
NOUN

Breaking news coming out of _____! It appears
PLACE

that Shane Gray, member of the hot band Connect Three, has

found _____ among the _____.
NOUN   PLURAL NOUN

After his label sent him to _____ to cool down,
SAME PLACE

he fell head over _____ for a mystery
PLURAL NOUN

voice. It wasn't until the famous Final Jam though, that he

_____ her. This previously unknown
VERB (PAST TENSE)

talent, Mitchie Torres, is destined to become a household

_____. Just wait and _____.
NOUN   VERB

Keep reading,

_____
CELEBRITY

Editor-in-Chief, *Star Scoop*

Found the Voice

Well _____,
NAME OF PERSON IN ROOM

I _____ the voice! And it was exactly

VERB (PAST TENSE)

who I had secretly _____ it would be—

VERB (PAST TENSE)

Mitchie! When I heard her singing up onstage, it was like a

_____ went off in my head. Her voice was so

NOUN

_____ and her lyrics so _____. I

ADJECTIVE   ADJECTIVE

couldn't help myself, I _____ on the stage

VERB (PAST TENSE)

and started singing with her. It was _____. I

ADJECTIVE

can't wait to _____ what the future holds!

VERB

Happily ever after?

Shane

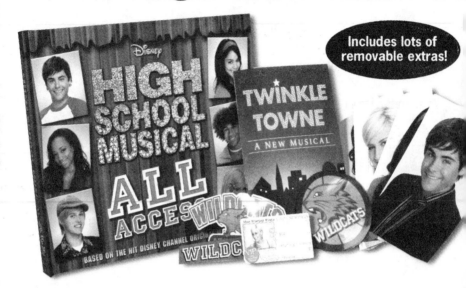